The Dynasty of Oghuz
Seljuk Empire and Ottoman Empire

Mohim Baig

Surah 1-Al-Fatihah (The Opening) – Al Quran

Bismillah-ir-Rahman-ir-Raheem

In the name of Allah, Most Gracious, Most Merciful.

Al Hamdu Lillaahi Rabbil Aalameen

Praise be to Allah, The Cherisher and Sustainer of the Worlds;

Ar Rahmaanir Raheem

Most Gracious, Most Merciful;

Maaliki Yaumid Deen

Master of the Day of Judgment

Iyyaaka Na Budu Wa Iyyaaka Nasta Een

You (alone) we worship, and you (alone) we ask for help (for each and everything).

Ihdinaas Siraatal Mustaqeem

Show us the straight way,

Siraatal Lazeena An Amta Alayhim Ghayril Maghdul Bi Alayhim Wa Laad Daalleen (Ameen)

The way of those on whom you have bestowed your Grace, those whose (portion) is not wrath, and who go not astray.

Bismillah-ir-Rahman-ir-Raheem

In the name of Allah, The Most Gracious and The Most
Merciful

Iqra Bismi Rab Bikal Lazee Khalaq
Read in the name of thy lord and cherisher who created

Khalaqal Insaana Min 'Alaq
Created man out of a (mere) clot of congealed blood

Iqra Wa Rab Bukal Akram
And thy lord is most bountiful

Al Lazee 'Allama Bil Qalam
He who taught (the use of) pen

'Al Lamal Insaana Ma Lam Y'alam
Taught man that which he knew not
Amabad

Surah Al-Alaq 96
Verse 12345
Al-Quran

In the name of Allah,
The Most Gracious and
The Most Merciful

Imaan – Believe in faith
Insaaf – Truth and Justice
Muhabbat – Love

About the Author

I was born in Baigor Bury Muslimabad (Deka Pur), Sylhet, East Pakistan (now Bangladesh). I came to England in 1973 with my parents and was brought up in England. After finishing high school, I worked in the family business and later ran my own partnership business from 1983-1993. I now work for a security company in Cambridge.

I enjoy serving the public and meeting them in social time. My research into several areas began in 1995 at various libraries, and my main interests are geography, history and culture, looking at nationalities, places, and peoples. I took a break from 2001 and recently restarted in 2018.

Most recently, I have been studying the Seljuk and Ottoman Empire and the Oghuz dynasties from 1037-1923. This is a large subject, which one cannot complete. My research and study have looked at the main aspects of their history and architecture, art and identity, and their way of life. I consider this civilization to be the most advanced in social and organizational development (1037-1923).

Mohim Baig

(Author)

Special Thanks

A special thanks to those who shared support toward this book

- Aadilah Asiyah Baig
- Abdul Karim Begh
- Abdul Quddus Begh
- Abdul Sufan Begh
- Akbar Baig
- Alec Pendred
- Alex Thomson
- Aleya Baig Hussain
- Amelia Amannah Baig
- Arif Hussain
- Azharul Imad Islam
- Ferducera Sara Baig
- Firdusi Sultana Baig
- Hannah Choudhary
- Harun Beg
- Hasna Baig
- Heeron Beg
- Ilyaas Choudhary
- Janhangir Begh
- Jasmin Tamzin
- Jessica Wijemini
- Joshua Woodrow
- Katie Wijesinghe
- Khadijah Baig
- Khaled Baig
- Khanum Baig Islam
- Lydia Alma Knight
- Maria Alexadra Bodea
- Marzana Islam
- Mihai Ciutureanu
- Mirza Imran Baig
- Mizan Begh
- Mohammad Liton Begh
- Nishath Anzoom Islam
- Olivia Hutton
- Omar Beg
- Rubaiya Yasmin Baig
- Sadhia Islam
- Saim
- Sameera Weeratunga
- Selon Begh
- Shagorika Baig
- Shumon Begh
- Sonny Baig
- Srishti Tyagi
- Suleiman Begh
- Suman Begh
- Tareeq Aziz Begh
- Yaqub Baig
- Yazan Eida
- Zaynab Baig
- Zora Baig
- Shah Rahman.
- Afruz Miah

- Mahboob Baig

Table of Contents

Contents

Chapter 1

Oghuz Khan

Have you heard the story of Noah? The great flood that came during his period and took with itself most of the human population? Only a few, who were the followers of Noah, could survive the great flood. However, the human race was revived again from these people who had survived; hence approximately 90% of the current population relates to Noah.

Noah had four sons in a total of which one drowned and died in flood. The rest of the three sons were Haem, Sham and Japheth. However, humanity was spread again in the world through these three sons. They are considered the forefathers of the population residing in the three main continents, including Europe, Africa and Asia.

Exploring the history and digging it further, I found out that Oghuz Khan, who Turks consider their forefather, is a descendent of Japheth (one of the surviving sons of Noah). After he survived the flood, he had moved to the East-Western part. Japheth had eight sons named Turk, Khazar, Saqlab, Rus, Ming, Chin, Kemeri and Tarik. Turk settled at Issiq Kul and was succeeded by Tutek, the eldest of his four sons. Four generations after him came two sons: Tatar and Mongol.

The period of Oghuz Khan dates back to even before Christ's birth, the Prophet Isaiah. The first amazing fact is that the period of Oghuz Khan travels back even before the birth of Christ, the Holy Prophet Isaiah (AS). According to Abu Al-Ghazi and Rashid Al-Din, a man called Ananja Khan belonged to Oghuz Khan's fifth generation. He had twin sons- one was called Tatar, and the other was Mongols. The empire of the Turk ancestor was split into two parts by both his sons. So, after these two grandchildren of Turk, the Barbarians (Tatar) tribes came into being. Both tribes were situated in areas that are known as Uzbekistan, Kyrgyzstan and Tajikistan today.

Talking about the descendants of Mongols, he had four sons named Kur Khan, Ur Khan, Qir Khan, and Qara Khan. As time passed, they all started to move away from the teachings of Islam and the oneness of Allah. During that period, Qara khan was blessed with a male child who was named Oghuz Khan.

Oghuz Han/Khan

Remember that it was the time before Christ, and people did not believe in God. Oghuz Khan was born to the principal wife of Qara Khan. Before he was born, Oghuz appeared in his mother's dream. In that dream, he told his mother, ' *If you do not believe in God, then I will not suckle from your breast'*.

She saw the same dream for three days until she was convinced that it was a sign for her and accepted her belief in God. However, she decided to keep it a secret as he was one of the greatest enemies of Islam and would have killed her after knowing that she had accepted the Oneness of God.

Some historians narrate this incident not as Oghuz Khan appearing in her mother's dream to tell her to accept the Oneness of God, but told her this after he was born. According to Abu al-Ghazi, when Oghuz Khan was born, he refused to drink his mother's milk. Even as a baby, he was able to speak and told her mother that he would not drink her milk until she accepted the one and true God.

Oghuz Khan had proved himself to be a special child since day one. He could talk even when he was a baby since the day he was born. He only drank his mother's milk for the first day, and the very next day, he asked his mother to feed him the milk of a mare (female horse) and meat. Just after 40 days after his birth, Oghuz Khan could walk like an adult. He had matured, both mentally and physically, much faster than any other child.

He grew into an adult much faster. It was indeed a sign that he was born to serve a purpose that will make him stand out among others. It was God's will. If God (Allah) wants to give his bounty to whom he likes-if, he says to be, it will be. Allah is everlasting. Allah is Raheem and Rahman, merciful and the most gracious.

So, when Oghuz Khan was born, the Turks were afraid of a giant dragon, Kiyant. It preyed on Turks and killed them. So, Oghuz took it upon himself to kill that dragon and provide the fellow Turks with the chance to live a life without the fear of being preyed upon that dragon.

One day, he took all his weapons and armed himself with all that he needed to accomplish this mission. First, he decided to set a trap for the dragon. For that, he took a freshly killed deer on a tree for the dragon to find it. Once the dragon fell for that trap, Oghuz took his bronze lance and cut off his head using his steel sword. After that incident, he was declared a hero.

冒顿单于
(Modu Chanyu)
Mete (Oğuz Kağan)

Oghuz Han/Khan

Oghuz Han/Khan- Marriages

As he grew older, he got married to one of the daughters of his uncle Kur Khan.
He also did a second marriage with the daughter of another uncle, Qir Khan.
Both these marriages were arranged. None of these marriages could survive
longer as his wives refused to embrace Islam and Oghuz decided to leave them.
His third marriage that was arranged with the daughter of his uncle Ur Khan
proved to be successful. His third wife was faithful to him. She agreed to
embrace Islam as she was willing to follow the same path as her husband's.

The whole tribe was against Islam, and when they got to know about them embracing Islam, they wanted to execute the husband and wife. Along with the whole tribe, his father wanted to kill them too. Finally, they reached the tent where Oghuz Khana and his wife. Oghuz Khan fought with all who were against him. He did not hesitate to raise his sword against his father when it came to defending his religion. He succeeded in executing his father in the fight, which was his first fight for Islam.

Given his courage to stand against the enemy and his efforts for Islam, Oguz Han/Khan is considered the mythological founder of the Turkic people and ancestor of the Oguz sub-branch of Turks. Even today, sub-branches of Oguz are classified in order of his six sons and 24 grandsons. Abu-Al- Ghazi writes about the lineage, Tamgha seal, signs, symbols, spirit guiding birds related to Oghuz Khan. In addition to these, he also identifies and specifies the political hierarchy and seating order at banquets for the six sons and 24 grandsons.

Oghuz Khan Legacy

Oghuz was blessed with three sons, and he celebrated this happiness by hosting a great feast. Then, he invites all the prominent and influential members of the tribe, his Beys/Begs (commanders or generals), and announced to them:

"I have become your Khan (leader). Let's all take swords and shields. Kut (divine power) will be our sign. Gray wolf will be our Uran (battle cry). Our iron lances will be a forest. Khulan will walk on the hunting ground. More seas and more rivers. Sun is our flag, and the sky is our tent."

He wanted the kings of the countries, from each corner of the world, to know of his position and power. Therefore, to spread his message and make his intention clear, he wrote letters to them that said:

"I am Khan of the Turks, and I will be Khan of all corners of the Earth. I want your obedience."

One of the recipients of his letters was Altun (Golden) Khan, who reigned at the right corner of the Earth. He submitted his obedience to Oghuz Khan as asked in the letter. However, Urum (Roman) Khan, whose reign was at the left corner of the Earth, did not submit. In response to his denial to submit, Oguz Khan declared war on Urum Khan. He gathered his army to fight against him and marched to the West. One night during his journey, he was staying in his tent while fighting against Urum; he was encountered with a strange being. A large wolf with grey fur, an avatar of the Tengri, came to his tent in an aura of light radiating from it. The wolf said to Oghuz,

'Oguz, you are marching on Urum; I will march before your army'.

And as it had declared, the grey sky wolf marched before the Turkish army and guided them. The two armies fought near the river Itil (Volga), and Oguz came out victorious in the war against Urum. After this successful fight, Oguz and his six sons then carried out campaigns in Turkistan, India, Iran, Egypt, Iraq and Syria. The grey wolf remained with them, guiding them through wars and helped Oghuz Khan become the Khan of the four corners of the Earth.

One of the significant incidents from Oghuz Khan's life that he shared with his sons was of him breaking a golden bow into three pieces. He then gave each of those pieces to his three oldest sons, Gun, Ay and Yildiz. After handing them the pieces, he addressed his oldest sons;

"My oldest sons, take this bow and shoot your arrow to the sky'.

Then he took out three silver arrows and handed them over to his three youngest sons; Gok, Dag and Deniz. Handing them the arrows, he addressed his youngest three sons;

"A bow shoots arrows, and you are like the arrow."

Then he addressed all of them, saying,

"My sons, I have walked a lot and seen many battles. I threw so many arrows and lances, rode many horses, made my enemies cry, made my friends smile, I paid my debt to Allah (God). Now I am giving my land to you."

With that, Oghuz Khan handed over his land and reign in the hands of his six sons, who carried the name of Oghuz Khan to the next generations that came after them.

Seal of Oguz Kagan

Statue of the great Oghuz Han/Khan

Oghuz Han 6 sons and 24 Grandsons tribes

List of Oghuz Dynasties

- Oguz Yabqu State
- Pecheneqs
- Seljuks
- Zengid Dynsaty
- Anatolian Beyliks
- Khwarazmian Dynasty
- Ottomans
- Aq Ooyunlu
- Kara Koyunlu
- Afsharids
- Qajars

Chapter 2

The Seljuk Empire

The Oghuz tribes dwelt in the mountain range of Altai or Altay, in the surrounding areas of Siberia, Russia, China, Mongolia and Kazakhstan, where the river Irtysh comes together and has its headwaters.

Seljuk Bey

Seljuk was one of the 24 tribes of Oghuz and belonged to the Turk branch, Kinik (Qiniq). The name of the Seljuk tribe is prominent among the rest of the tribes because it was the first to establish a government in Asia Minor. The house of Seljuk lived on the north of the Caspian and Aral seas. The location of their homeland was on the periphery of the Muslim world. Around the 10th century, the house of Seljuks migrated to Khorasan and then into mainland Persia. They settled there and adopted the language and culture of Persia in the following years. The house of Seljuk was led by chieftain or Bey- the traditional ancestor of Seljuk, Seljuk. Seljuk was reputed to be an army officer who served the Khazar army.

Seljuk Bey
Died 1007-1009 (Age 100-107)

Around 610 A.D., a new faith was born, called Islam. At the time, the Sasanian Empire was Persian, and the Byzantine Empire was Christian. As time passed by, Islam began to spread fast and eventually became a fast-spreading religion. Around AD 983, the Buyid leader Fana Khusrau became the first ruler of Islamic Persia and took the title of Shahanshah- the King of Kings.

Seljuk Bey then migrated from Kirgiz steppes to Bursa. When Seljuks settled there, they converted to Islam. This was where Seljuk Empire was established. Seljuk bey had four sons; Arsalan Isra'il, Mikhail, Musa Yabgu and Younus. Seljuk Bey's son Mikhail Bey had two sons; Tugrul Bey and Chagri Bey. After the death of his son Mikhail, Seljuk took care of his two grandsons. Seljuk Bey died at the age of 107. Seljuk Bey's elder son then took over the lead but eventually, he became too embroiled in the politics of the region and got arrested due to some political issues.

Muhammad Ghaznavid had a significant role in the emergence of Seljuks in history as a powerful entity. He aided the Seljuks and granted them permission to settle in the region. In return, he asked them for tributes. Once settled, the Seljuks managed to take their roots on the land and cement their power over time. When Sultan Ghaznavid died in 1030 C.E, his son Mas'ud took over his reign. He had difficulty dealing with the redoubtable subjects and was eventually defeated in the famous battle near Hirat. This event had a significant impact on the power of Seljuks in that region. They got more powerful, and that was when Tugrul, one of the Seljuk's grandsons, ascended to power.

Tugrul Bey

Under his rule, Tugrul established the very first Seljuk State. The State under his rule occupied the whole of Persia. At first, the capital of the State was Nishanpur, but it later changed to Konya. Both Tugrul and his brother played their part to run the State, while Tugrul took over the more significant matters of the State, his brother Chagri Bey governed over Khorasan from 1040 through 1060 AD.

Tugrul Bey
1037-1063

With the combined efforts of Tugrul and his brother Chagri, they took over Marw and Naysabar and took power from the Ghaznavids, who occupied these regions. As time passed, Tugrul Bey's accomplishment got rapid, and soon, he managed to sway several regions, including Khwarizm, Tabaristan, Hamdhan, Balkh, Jurjan, and Isbahan.

These were the times when Tugrul's rule had started to overpower the influence of Buwayhids in Persia, and at the same time, the Abbasid Caliph Qadir bi Allah breathed his last. After his death, his son Abu Ja'far 'Abd Allah succeeded to the throne. He was given the title of al-Qaim. At that very time, Tugrul had taken over the surroundings of Baghdad. Sometime later, by compulsion, Calip Al-Qaim asked Tugrul to meet him. He had some critical decisions to make. Tugrul was received by Al-Qaim. When Tugrul went to meet him, he was sitting at a platform, and a curtain was draped in front of him. The drape was lifted when Tugrul Bey approached him. The Caliph offered Tugrul to sit on an adjoining platform. And then, Tugrul was hailed as the regent of the empire by Al-Qaim. Along with that, Tugrul has also bestowed the title of al-Sultan. After that, Tugrul Bey had proclaimed himself as Sultan in the capital of Caliph. Assuming his sovereign power, Tugrul Bey read his name in official prayers or Kutba prayers held every Friday in the Great Mosque in Baghdad.

During Tugrul's Sultanate, a Turkish chief named Arsalan al-Basasiri tried to seize the power of the Buwayhid ruler from the palace and wanted to replace their position at the office of Amir al-Umra. He got succeeded in his mission. At that time, Tugrul Bey had been away for an expedition. Taking advantage of his absence, Arsalan al-Basasiri compelled al Qaim to sign documents stating that he is renouncing all his rights in favour of the Fatimids of Cairo.

Once al-Basasiri got the documents signed, he sent the emblems of the Caliphate to Egypt like the pulpit, sceptre, mantle, etc. After that, In the Masjid of Iraq, there were prayers recited in the name of Fatimid. The news reached Tugrul Bey. As soon as he heard about it, he hurried back to Baghdad. He encountered al-Basasiri, defeated and killed him. Once dealing with al-Basasiri, he reinstated caliph al-Qaim on his rightful throne in 1060 C.E.

Alp Arsalan

Tugrul Bey died in AD 1063. After him, Alp Arsalan succeeded Tugrul Bey on August 26th 1071. He was the son of Chagri Bey and nephew of Tugrul Bey. He fought the battle of Manzikert and defeated the Byzantine Army in Anatolia. His victory in this battle marked the beginning of a new era in the Turkish world. After he won the battle, Emperor Romanos under whom the Byzantine fought against Seljuks, was captured and brought to the presence of Alp Arsalan. Alp Arsalan had a conversation with him.

The conversation between them went on like:

Alp Arsalan said;

"What would you do if I was brought before you as a prisoner, Romanos?"

To that, the Emperor replied;

"Perhaps I would kill you or exhibit you in the streets of Constantinople (now Istanbul).'

Alp Arsalan replied to him;

"My punishment is much heavier; I forgive you and set you free."

Alp Arsalan chose to treat the Emperor with generosity. He had set him free after peace terms were agreed. Once agreed, Alp Arsalan dismissed the Emperor respectfully along with many gifts.

Alp Arsalan Bey
1063-1072

Malik Shah-Son of Alp Arsalan Bey
1072-1092

Alp Sultan was the second Seljuk Sultan who reigned over Seljuk Empire after Tugrul. Under his rule, he made efforts to expand the territory and consolidate power. He succeeded in his mission by defeating his rivals in both his South and North. During one of his campaigns in 1072, Alp Arsalan sustained some fatal wounds during a fight. Succumbing to his injuries, he died in 1072. After that, his son, Malik Shah, was crowned the new Sultan a few days later and became the third Sultan of the Seljuk Empire.

The history of Seljuks and the establishment of their empire are rich, full of battles and accomplishments. Seljuks were the first Turkish dynasty that ruled the Muslim world and revived the dying Caliphate at that time. When they arrived from their homeland, it marked the beginning of fresh inspiration for Muslims, religious devotion and a true example of strong leadership.

The period of Seljuk reign reflects the desire that they had for decorative activities and architecture. They played a significant role in the development of architecture in the 11th century, representing the Muslim world. The architectural heritage came from the Assanian and Abbasid Madrasa Koranic School, whose architectural traditions were followed to the Masjid with Persian style courtyards. This Madrasa was developed during the era of Seljuks. Recently converted Turks spread the Madrasa as a means of re-establishing Orthodox Sunnism.

Seljuks managed to maintain their rule for around 157 years. It was established in 1037 and dissolved down in 1194

Seljuk Flag

Chapter 3

Nasir Salah Ad-Din Yusuf Ibn Ayyub

Islamic history is full of brave Ghazis who devoted their lives to Islam and their people. Among these, Salahuddin is one of the most prominent names. Salahuddin's full name was An-Naseer Salah Ad-Din Yusuf who was the son of Najim Ad-din Ayyub. He is known to be a great warrior of Islam. He was born in 1137 AD in Tikrit, which is now known as Iraq. His name was Yusuf; however, he was also given the name Salahuddin- an honorific laqab (epithet) that means "Righteousness of the Faith".

He was born into a Sunni-Kurdish family that had originated from the village of Ajdanakan in central Armenia. Salahuddin was strongly influenced by a famous scholar of that time, Sheikh Abdul Qadir Gilani. He studied the Quran (the holy book of Muslims), mathematics, theology, and law. His uncle Asad-ad-Din Shirkoh was a commander of the Zengid Dynasty- a Muslim dynasty that of Oghuz Turkic origin that ruled the parts of Upper Mesopotamia and Levant under the command of the Seljuk Empire.

Salahuddin was trained by his uncle and had become a part of the military. He had shown his capabilities a number of times, leading him to take on the leading responsibilities during several military campaigns. His progress did not just remain limited to the military. His cleverness, sharp mindedness and great tactics allowed him to become the Sultan of both Syrian and Egypt. He started as a soldier and ended up ruling over two great countries.

Salahuddin's name is not only known in the Islamic world. Salahuddin was one of the most famous Muslim historical figures in the West and is known as Saladin. He left his mark wherever he went and built his reputation as a military leader under the rule of the Shi'a Fatimid Caliphate who had established built Cairo. With his accomplishments, he managed to become head of the military force in 1169. Later, he was made the advisor to the Shi'ite caliph in Cairo. As the time passed, he continued to prove his capabilities and power as he eliminated the Fatimid's sub-Saharan infantry slave forces. But, as time passed, Salahuddin took over that Caliphate's power and was able to seize it in 1171. Once, he managed to do that and marked the beginning of a new era. After taking over the throne, Salahuddin began his efforts for the foundation of the Ayyubi Dynasty in 1137. He succeeded and became the very first Sultan of both Syria and Egypt.

Nasir Salahuddin Yusuf Ibn e Ayyub

(Salahdin)

It was his faith in his religion and firm values, along with his determination to devote his life to the Islamic cause that he never hesitated to take a step forward and accomplish great things during his reign.

Salahuddin's reputation as Saladin in the West was established during the Third Crusade. He led the Muslim armies to the West and fought against Richard I of England. His behaviour and leadership had been so inspiring that despite being defeated, the Europeans admired him for his courageous and chivalrous behaviour during his campaign against them. That eventually earned him the respect of the Crusaders and their Leader, Richard I. His most notable act during Third Crusade was that he granted amnesty to the Crusaders and the Christians of Jerusalem. It was when he took the city back in 1187 AD in return for a very small ransom.

Salahuddin was a warrior who freed Jerusalem from the Crusaders. Despite being in a war, he chose to be honourable and gallant. He was a living example of the tolerant, progressive and inclusive faith Islam, which was dear to his heart. By showing restraint and peaceful behaviour, he upheld the central tenants of Islam, such as freedom of religion and protection of non-Muslims.

For 20 years, he stood up against the crusaders and eventually drove them away. After Salahuddin, the world has rarely seen a more gallant and compassionate conqueror. His combat strategies were unrivalled. Salahuddin is often regarded as the ideal warrior, ferocious in combat but kind to his opponents. Salahuddin used to offer the five obligatory prayers punctually. He always prayed in the congregation, and he never delayed his prayer. He was constantly accompanied by an Imam. Except for three days before his death, he never stopped praying when he slipped into a coma.

Salahuddin has become a symbol of resistance to the Western world in Arab and Islamic history, particularly after the development of Arab nationalism in the 20th century. The Egyptian flag has Saladin's Eagle as a crest in the middle. You can also find Salahuddin's physical legacy in Cairo. The finest example is the building of Cairo's Citadel, which has been named after him as the Salah Ad-Din Citadel, and the expansion walls of the city that were supposed to be constructed under Salahuddin's rule but not were completed until after he died in 1193 AD.

Egypt and Syria were unified by the Ayyubid Empire of Salah Ad-Din. In his victorious recapture of Jerusalem, which helped him gain his reputation in both Muslim and Western history, he played a significant part in fighting the Crusaders. While one may anticipate that Crusaders must have detested Salahuddin that was not the case. Due to his chivalry and kindness to the Christians, he became one of the esteemed Muslim figures of the Medieval Islamic world.

Chapter 4

The Byzantine Empire

The Byzantine Empire is also called Byzantium or Eastern Roman Empire. It was a Christian state and its official language was Greek. This great Empire existed from 330-1453 and is known to be the longest-lasting medieval power. Its capital was founded by Constantine I at Constantinople (r. 306-337). The size of this empire varied throughout its existence as the empire grew over the centuries, possessing the territories located in different areas including Greece, Asia Minor, North Africa, The Balkans, Levant and Italy.

Some of the Byzantine Emperors

The Byzantines had developed their own system to run the empire including religious practices and political systems. Their art and architecture, however, was greatly influenced by Greco-Roman cultural tradition. It was distinct but certainly was not merely the continuation of ancient Rome. Even after the end of this empire, its influence continued and even today, its influence can be witnessed in the law, architecture, art and religion in many states of the West, Russia, East and Central Europe.

Byzantium was the first name of the capital before it was changed to Constantinople which is now called Istanbul. Based on this fact, 16th-century historians coined the name "Byzantine". It serves as a convenient label to differentiate between the Western Roman Empire and Eastern Roman Empire, especially after the fall of the Western Roman Empire in the 5th century. For this reason alone, the actual period of the time that the "Byzantine Empire" refers to is still disputed.

Some of the disputed dates and years among the historians regarding this empire are mentioned below:

- You will find some historians selecting 330 for the foundation of Constantinople.
- Some agree on the fall of the Western Roman Empire in 476.
- Some agree on the failure of Justinian I (r. 527-565) as the reason behind the unification of the two empires in 565.
- You will also find some of the historians plumping for c. 650 when the Arabs took over the Byzantine's eastern provinces.
- One date that most historians agree on is Tuesday 29 May 1453, when Byzantine Empire terminated and Ottoman Sultan Mehmed II (r.1444-6 & 1451-81) conquered Constantinople.

These dates not only shed light on the significant incidents and events throughout the history of this empire but also the cultural and ethnic mix between two different halves of the Roman world. In addition to that, it also highlights how distinct the medieval state was from its earlier Roman heritage.

Whether the Byzantines were Romans or Greeks can be confusing. The Byzantines called themselves 'Romans', however, the most common language spoken by them was Greek. Their capital was the New Rome and their emperor was BASILEON TON RHOMAION or 'Emperor of the Romans'. With their linkage with both Roman and Greek roots, it is quite confusing to some people to understand whether the Byzantines were Romans or Greeks. But if people dig into the history and explore it in detail, they will know that the Byzantine Empire was without any doubt, was more Greek than Roman in cultural terms.

Constantinople (Modern Istanbul) - the beginning of the Byzantine Empire

On 11th May 330, the Roman Emperor Constantine I decided to relocate the capital of the Roman Empire from Rome to Byzantium. This marked the beginning of the great Byzantine Empire. The name emperor chose for this new capital was "New Rome which was later changed to the popular name Constantinople (City of Constantine), replacing the emperor's choice of name.

Constantine I

One of the most important aspects of this capital was its natural harbour on the Golden Horn inlet. A chain also stretched the entrance of the Golden Horn. This harbour straddled the border between Asia and Europe. This gave the harbour the control over the passage of ships that would go through the Bosporus- a link that promoted lucrative trades between east and west.

Between 410 and 413, a great wall named *"Theodosian Walls"* was constructed around the city which was strong enough to withstand attack from both land and the sea. As time passed, more buildings and spectacular architecture were added to this city, making it one of the greatest and richest Christian cities in the world that has not lost its charm till today.

The Emperors of Byzantine

BASILEON TON RHOMAION (in rare cases, a BASILISSA if the ruler was an empress) or the Emperor of Byzantine used to live in the Great Palace of Constantinople. These emperors ruled the Great Byzantine Empire as the absolute monarchs. The emperor or the *basileus,* however, require the assistance of a widespread bureaucracy an expert government. An emperor of the Byzantine Empire was an absolute ruler and had the power to make decisions on his own. However, the government, people and the Church expected the emperor or the empress to rule wisely and justly.

Byzantine depiction of Justinian in Ravenna, Italy

The most important characteristic that an emperor was expected to have by his people and his government was military success. It was indeed a sign of power and remained one in Byzantium in real terms. Any emperor who was not able to defend the empire or failed to keep the economy from a catastrophe could be removed by the mutual decisions made by the army generals and the provinces. But if the vents went by normal and everything was run perfectly by the emperor, the emperor was the head of the Church, Commander-in-Chief of the army and well as the head of the government. Also, the emperors were in charge of managing and controlling the finances of the States, had the authority for the appointment and dismissal of the nobles at will.

There were several customs and practices that helped the reign of this great empire and continued to exude a strong influence on the world. The rulers had a carefully orchestrated continuation of dynasties that were backed by strong and influential names, rituals and customs that helped the institution of the emperors to last for 12 centuries.

Byzantine Government

The pattern followed by the Byzantine government was similar to the one established in Imperial Rome. The emperor had all the power, however; the consultation of the important bodies of the society such as the Senate was important. The elites in the Senate constituted a small SACRUM CONSISTORIUM who consulted on the matters of the state.

The *Praetorian Prefect of the East* was, however, the top officials in Byzantine. The regional governors were accountable to the members of *the Praetorian Prefect.* The councils of the government were distributed geographically into approximately 100 provinces. These provinces were arranged into 12 dioceses. These dioceses were divided into the empire's four prefectures, three in each prefecture.

In the 7th century, the provincial military commander (strategoi), who was directly accountable to the emperor, or themes as it was known after the reorganization, became the provincial prefect. After the 8th century, the empire's administration was considerably easier than before, due to the increasing military threat from neighbours and civil conflicts.

Byzantine Emperor surrounded by his household troops

The Byzantine Empire Territories

Military success and failures of the individual emperors had an impact on the geographical extent of the Byzantine Empire. That's why; it changed over the course of time and fluctuated with the succession of each emperor. In the earlier part of Byzantine history, the territory included Jordan, Syria, Lebanon, Palestine and Egypt.

Greece on the other hand, always had a significant value for the Byzantines in practical terms as it was a symbol of how they viewed themselves; the true heirs of Greco-Roman culture. The Byzantines also struggled to defend Italy and Sicily from the ambitions of Normans and the Popes. However, they were unsuccessful in this regard.

Balkans up to the Danube River, Asia Minor up to the Black Sea coast in the north and Armenia in the east were very important territories for the prosperity of the Byzantine Empire as these areas were the major source of wealth. However, they required both regular and vigorous defence against various enemies surrounding these territories.

Later in the 7th and 8th centuries, the Islamic conquests began. During this time, Islamic leaders made their way to Byzantine Empire and took over its territories including the Levant, eastern Asia Minor and North Africa and also Jerusalem in 637. The Byzantine Empire maintained to stand firm against the Arab sieges (674-8 and 717-18). However, the foundation of the Empire had been shaken from this encounter with the Arabs.

During his reign, Basil I (r. 867-886) managed to reconquer southern Italy and also came out victorious against the Arabs on mainland Greece, Cyprus and Dalmatia. The emperor who took the reign after he was Leo VI (r. 886-912) who lost almost all the gains of Basil I. In the mid-10th century, the Byzantines took control over Mesopotamia that in the control of Muslims.

Basil II (r. 976-1025) was another emperor who ruled the Byzantine Empire and was also called 'Bulgar-Slayer' for his victories and gains in the Balkans. Basil also managed to gain victories in Syria, Armenia, Greece and Georgia. He managed to take over these new territories and doubled the size of the Byzantine Empire with the help of a fierce army of Vikings. However, it was the last of the greatest victory that the Byzantine Empire had seen during its existence. After these victories, the Empire saw a gradual decline. The foundation of the Empire was further weakened by the shocking defeat to the Seljuks at the Battle of Manzikert that took place in Armenia in 1071.

After that battle, the Empire managed a brief revival under the rule of Alexios I Komnenos (r. 1081-1118). He managed to credit several victories to his name when he took down the Pechenegs in Thrace and Normans in Dalmatia. He also defeated the Seljuks in Palestine and Syria with the help of the first crusaders. However, despite all the victories, the Byzantine Empire could not prosper indefinitely into its former glory as there were too many enemies surrounding the Empire.

In the 12th and 13th centuries, half of Asia Minor was taken over by the Sultanate of Rum. Following that, the armies of the Fourth Crusade attacked

Constantinople in 1204. These vents led the Byzantine Empire to only exist in exile and carved up between Venice and its other allies. By the beginning of the 14th century, the Byzantine Empire covered only a small area in southern Greece, including a small area around the capital. Then in 1453, the fall of this great Empire finally took place when the attack on Constantinople from the Ottomans proved to be a final blow to the falling Empire of Byzantine.

Chapter 5

Seljuk and Byzantine Wars

The history is filled with a series of decisive battles between Byzantine and Seljuk. The Byzantine-Seljuk wars continually shifted the balance of power in Syria and Asia Minor, starting from the Byzantine Empire to the Seljuk Turks. When the Suljuks arrived from the steppes of Central Asia, they had learned to replicate the tactics that were practiced by the Huns hundreds of years before. The Huns used those tactics against the Romana opponents, similar to the ones that Seljuks encountered. However, the Seljuks combined those tactics with the new-found Islamic zeal that they had developed after embracing Islam. Using their new, developed tactics, they used them in many ways and resumed with their Muslims conquest in the Byzantine—Arab Wars that were initiated by the Abbasid Caliphate, Umayyad and Rashidun in the Asia Minor, North Africa and Levant.

The Battle of Manzikert

The most remarkable battle that took between the Seljuk Turks and the Byzantines was the Battle of Manzikert. That battel is seen as the moment in history when the great Byzantine Empire lost the war against Seljuk Turks. However, before 1071, the military force of the Byzantine Empire was of questionable quality. The frequent incursions from the Turks overran the failing theme system of the Byzantine Empire. However, this great empire did not fall immediately. It stood firm for several years before it fell. The Turks kept the heavy concessions on the Byzantines that eventually resulted in the fall of Byzantine Empire. But it is important to note that it took Turks another 20 years before they could get the control of Anatolia. But their control did not last long either.

As the war between Seljuks and Byzantines went on, the Seljuk Turks had other opponents as well. Seljuks, along with their allies, catalyzed the call for the first Crusade as well as attacked the Fatimid Caliphate of Egypt. Byzantine had acquired the assistance of the Crusaders. Their endeavors were filled with treachery and looting, and they had made substantial gains in the first Crusade.

During the hundred years of Manzikert, Byzantine, along with the assistance of Crusaders, were successful in driving back the Seljuks from the coastal areas of Asia Minor. After this success, they were able to take over some control and had some influence over Egypt and Palestine. Later in the years after that, Byzantines were unable to acquire any further assistance that they needed. The Fourth Crusade led to the sack of Constantinople. Before this happened, Seljuks had taken over some of the territories of the weakened Empire of Nicaea. However, they could not take control over it completely as the Sultanate itself was taken down by the Mongols that resulted in the rise of the Ghazis and eventually, the conclusive Byzantine–Ottoman wars.

The Battle of Manzikert (1071)

The Byzantines had begun making their headway against the Arabs in 10th century. At that time, Ghaznavid ruled over Persia who were another group of Turkic people. When the Seljuks migrated to Persia in 10th century, it led to the end of Ghaznavid rule in Persia. The Seljuks had adopted the customs and culture of Persia after they settled there. Eventually, they grew in power and established their powerful domain there. From there, they continued and captured Baghdad in 1055 and overthrew the reign of Abbasid Caliphate. After that, the Abbasid just became a figurehead in the Islamic world. Seljuks continued with their conquests and spurred by their success in battles and attacks, they launched an attack on the Levant. This attack was against the Fatimid Egypt.

The Byzantine and Seljuks, however, did not encounter each other in wars until after the reign of Byzantine Emperor Basil II. But before their actual encounters, Seljuks did have some influence by the incursions of the Seljuk Turks into Georgia, over the outcomes of the other wars such as Byzantine-Georgian wars Byzantines were engaged in.

When the Seljuks attacked the Byzantines the first time, they were prepared to win. They had chosen the best time to attack as the Byzantine Empire was faced by the weak rule as well as the Norman Conquest and schism. The Abbasid Caliphate, on the other hand, had been weakened by their encounters with the Fatimid dynasty.

Since the beginning of 11th century, Seljuks had continued to expand their power towards the west. In the process, they had defeated several Arab factions and had taken over the Abbasid caliphate's reign in Baghdad. Meanwhile, Byzantine was busy in its own excursions towards Edessa and Syria and had managed to have some gains on these territories.

In the year 1067, the Seljuks had attacked the Caesarea during their invasion in Asia Minor. A few years later in 1069, they also attacked the Iconium. In the same year, the Byzantines counterattacked and drove the Seljuks back from these two areas. They did not stop at just that attack as they continued with their attacks and drove back the Seljuks back across the Euphrates.

But these attacks from the Byzantine did not affect the Seljuks and they continued their excursions. They continued with their invasion into Asia Minor and successfully managed to capture Manzikert. At that time, the Byzantine Empire was being ruled by Romanus Diogenes who attempted an attack on Seljuqs to add military justification to his rule (the government of Byzantine required the emperors to have some military success), as he his rule had already seem the loss of Southern Italy to Norman conquest.

Alp Arsalan- Reclaiming Manzikert

Under the leadership of Alp Arsalan, the Seljuks withdrew from Manzikert. It was a successful tactic that allowed his army to have a surprise attack on the Byzantines. It led the Seljuks to reclaim Manzikert. This victory turned out to be fruitful as it led to a few other gains for Seljuks. The civil chaos that had risen in the Byzantine Empire gave the Seljuks and other Turkic allies a perfect chance to invade the Asia Minor again.

Once the Seljuks had reclaimed Manzikert, they focused more on gaining the territories on the Eastern side that was, at that time, Fatimid dynasty in Egypt. Alp Arsalan had encouraged the other Turk allies nearby and vassals in order to establish Beylics in Asia Minor with the joined efforts.

At that time, the Byzantines could not see their victory as a complete failure. When Turks started to occupy the countryside in Anatolia, they also started to guard the cities of Byzantine with their troops. They did not take this step as the foreign Turk conquerors but as the mercenaries selected by several Byzantine factions themselves. One of the Byzantine emperors even decided to give the defense of the city to the Turks in 1078.

Byzantine Recruiting Turkic Assistance

As a consequence of the civil war, pretenders to the Byzantine Empire recruited Turkic assistance by relinquishing Byzantine territory. The loss of major cities like Nicaea and another setback in Anatolia resulted in an extended conflict. The civil strife was concluded when Alexius I, the ruler of the Imperial army in Asia Minor, declared himself a rebel, and claimed the Byzantine throne in the year 1081.

In 1084, Antioch and Smyrna were lost to emergency reforms carried out by Alexius I. During 1078 until 1084 the city was, however, in the control of the Armenian Renegade, Philaretos Brachamios. By 1091, Alexius inherited the very few surviving Byzantine towns in Asia Minor.

In the same year, 1091, the joint invasion of Seljuq and Pecheneg and the siege in Constantinople were successfully repelled by the Byzantines while Norman assaults had also been delayed so that the Byzantine Empire could concentrate its energy on the Turks. The Byzantines were therefore able to retrieve Tzachas the Aegean islands, destroy its navy and recapture the southern shore of the Marmara Sea even in 1094.

In 1094 Alexius Comnenus sent a letter seeking arms, equipment and skilled men from Pope Urban II. The Pope preached at the Clermont Council in 1095 about a Crusade to seize Jerusalem and, in this process, helped the Byzantine Empire which was no longer able to protect Christendom from Islamic warfare in the East. Although the Crusades did help the Byzantine Empire reconquer several important cities, in 1204, the Empire was dissolved. At that time, it had become difficult for the Byzantines to preserve their territory.

The First Crusaders

After Alexius' appeal to the west, the first Crusaders arrived in 1096. The Byzantine-Crusader agreement was to restore all the Byzantine towns that were to be re-captured from Turks to the empire. This was good for the Crusaders since they did not need to guard the seized cities and lose soldier strength while preserving their supply routes. The Byzantines, in exchange, would provide the Crusaders with food in a hostile region, according to the agreement. In perilous situations, the soldiers of Alexius would function as a backup. On 6 May 1097, the Crusaders attacked Nicaea for the first time in order to take their territory back.

On the 16th of May, another slight setback persuaded Kilij Arslan to retreat and give up Nicaea, which was handed up to the Byzantines on 19 June. He couldn't help Turks because of their enormous troops that Byzantines had acquired. He wasn't able to help and The Crusaders then won a decisive victory over Dorylaeum and openly attacked Asia Minor; Sozopolis, Philomelium, Iconium, Antioch in the city of Pisidia, Caesarea and Heraclea, all collapsed on to the Crusaders attack. They even reached Cilicia, where Armenians were freed from Turkish control and supply base was established.

Unfortunate for Byzantine, they were unable to benefit effectively from these victories during the reign of Alexius Comnenus, who had Caesarea returned to the Seljuq as part of the Sultanate of Rum together with a large number of other cities such as Iconium, the subsequently, the capital of the Seljuk Turks. In 1097, in the campaign that reestablished the strong Byzantine influence of the Aegean and several urban zones of western Anatolia and ended up taking the cities of Laodicea Smyrna, Ephesus and Philadelphia from the Turks who had been demoralized with a great deal of loss. The Mega Doukas, who was the brother-in-law of Alexius, helped guide both land-based and sea forces of the Byzantine in this campaign.

Stephen of Blois and Kerbogah

A picture depicting the siege of Antioch from the 15th century, with troops wearing plates in opposition to mail armor-The Crusaders subsequently launched a siege on the city of Antioch ruled by Seljuk after their conquests. By the command of Stephen of Blois, the siege ended with Crusader's help to the Byzantines. Kerbogah was a vassal of the Seljuks who had a force of 75,000 soldiers sent to relieve Antioch. He was unsuccessful in this mission to successfully besiege the Edessa, which had previously fallen to the Crusaders. This gave the Crusaders the time to conquer Antioch on June 3, 1098, just the day before Kerbogah arrived.

Nevertheless, Kerbogah soldiers managed to break the citadel, where fierce and desperate struggles permitted the Crusaders to repel his attack. However, Byzantine Emperor decided to back off when Stephen of Blois, one of the Crusaders present, deserted and Alexius Comnenus told him of the destruction of the Crusaders. As a consequence of this seeming abandonment of Alexius I, the Crusaders declined to return to Antioch after they succeed in defeating Kerbogah's dispersed army. The Crusaders abandoned their support for the Byzantines against the Seljuks and their allies due to resentment. A new Crusade of the first one was finished with utter defeat in 1101 and the strengthening of Seljuq's authority in Asia Minor with the foundation of the Iconium as the capital of the Rum Sultanate (known as Konya in the present day).

John II Comnenus came to power after the death of Alexius I. By now, the Seljuk Turks were broken and weakly linked to each other. The Sultanate of Rum fought during that period against its old allies known as the Danishmends. This was an advantage for the Byzantines, and John Comnenus took this opportunity and attempted a series of conflicts to recapture Anatolia. Under his leadership, the front line was pushed deep into Anatolia and reached the capital of his adversaries perilously near Iconium. However, in Anatolia, the Turks persisted in the battle against each other, but Emperor John was robbed of the chance to have a definitive victory by a terrible hunting accident.

The Battle of Myriokephalon

John II passed away in 1143 during a mighty Byzantine empire. The new emperor, Manuel Comnenus, could not expand his forefront beyond the accomplishments of his father. Under the leadership of Kilij Arslan II, the Seljuq Turks were able to defeat their opponents, the Danishmends. The Byzantines also fought against the Danishmends as Seljuk's nominal allies during that period. The agreement included a takeover of the Danishmend land by the Byzantines. Manuel Comnenus brought an astonishingly large force into Seljuq territory in 1176 in an attempt to take its capital city, the Iconium, after Kilij Arslan II refused to give the Byzantines their promised lands.

However, at a mountain pass, the Byzantine Force was ambushed with severe casualties on both sides. It was the battle of Myriokephalon that led to the abandonment of the Byzantine conquest campaign. Because of the nature of the conflict and the geography, the borders of Byzantine territory and the Sultanate of Iconium and the Four Emirates were frequently breached by raiding groups on both sides.

The Battle of Myriokephalon

The battle against each other between the two leaders who wanted peace was tactically indecisive. After this, the army of Manuel proceeded in a small but indecisive war against the Turks in Anatolia in the Meander Valley. Regardless of that being a small respite, Myriokephalon's impacts were considerably more crucial than the casualties indicated - the Asia Minor under Manuel Comnenus was no longer reconquered after 1176, such as that under his father's rule. The Seljuqs had their triumph over the acquisition of Danishmend land, but they had to struggle once more with the neighbouring differences resulting in a peace pact, as both leaders sought. Under the Treaty, Manuel was obligated to withdraw its soldiers and fortifications from the Dorylaeum and Sublaeum.

Battle of Hyelion and Leimocheir

Manuel Comnenus, however, refused to implement the treaty. When Kilij Arslan tried to implement this Treaty, the Byzantine Emperor sent John Vatatzes to repel the Turkish invasion. He managed to score a victory over the Turks in Meander Valley during the Battle of Hyelion and Leimocheir. It was a sign that the Byzantine army stayed strong and also that their defence system of Western Asia Minor was still successful. Instead, he refused to allow the Turkish invaders to be repelled. Manuel personally marched to expel the Turks from Panasium and Lacerium, southeast of Cotyaeum, with a small force after the Meander victory.

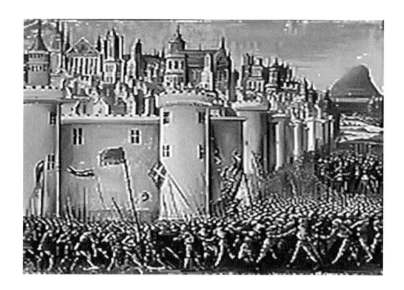

In 1178, however, after meeting a Turkish force in Charax, a Byzantine army retreated, which enabled the Turks to capture numerous livestock. The town of Claudiopolis in Bithynia was attacked by the Turks in 1179, and Manuel was forced to command a few cavalry forces to preserve the town. The Byzantines managed to achieve a victory over the Turks even as late as 1180.

Manuel's vitality was seriously affected by the conflict; his health decreased, and creeping fever came in 1180. Like Manzikert, the equilibrium between the two forces gradually began to change — Manuel was never assaulted by the Turks again, and the Turks continued to advance more profound into the Byzantine realm farther and west after Manuel's death.

Byzantine in turmoil

Manuel's death in 1180 did not discontinue the Komnenoi dynasty. Still, the son of Manuel proved to be unable to hold together an empire saddled with heavy expenditure due to the campaigns started by his father. The replacement for Alexis II Comnenus was Andronikos I of Komnenos, who took the throne in 1183. The Komnenos was also unsuccessful. His attempts to further militarize the empire resulted in his torture, blindness, public humiliation for three days and ultimately death in 1185. Sozopolis, Ankara and Heraclea all succumbed to Kilij Arslan II and finally resulted in the benefit for Myriokephalon.

The Byzantine Empire, which failed to protect its boundary after this instability, was governed by a number of corrupt or inept emperors from 1185 until 1204. The weakening Byzantine Imperial control led to the liberation of the Armenian Kingdom of Cilicia and Prince Leo II on the throne in 1187. Antioch was also freed from its Byzantine vassal status in 1180.

The Third Crusade- Byzantine Seeking help from Saladin

In Palestine, meanwhile, the Crusaders started falling to Saladin, which led to the Third Crusade. The Holy Roman Empire ended up with a wasted opportunity, and the Byzantine Empire made significant improvements in the Middle East. In a further demonstration of his incompetent rule, Saladin was promised by Emperor Isaac II to keep the Third Crusade from crossing Anatolia. Byzantine's military power under the rule of Isaac II, whose military was small to support this agreement. But he could not make use of the Iconium sack Crusaders that could overturn the setback at Myriokephalon when he allowed the Third Crusade to pass Anatolia due to Frederick I's threat.

Fourth Crusade

In 1204 the city of Constantinople was ravaged by troops of the Fourth Crusade, throwing the empire into another period of instability. The downfall of Byzantium became much more probable because the empire surrounded by enemies. The Seljuqs of Rum exploited this situation and, in 1207, invaded Antalya port from the weakened and divided Empire of Nicaea under the new Sultan, Kaykhusraw.

Battle of Antioch on the Meander

However, the tide turned in 1210, when the Emperor of Nicaea slew the Sultan himself in a single battle at the Meander Battle of Antioch. Since then, the Eastern frontier had become more or less stable. In 1243, Seljuq's dominance shattered in Anatolia with the invasion of the Mongols.

The three young sons of Kaykhusraw II were enthroned three years later, after the early death of Kaykhusraw II. Civil conflicts erupted in the sultanate of Rum once again that resulted in the Empire of Nicaea recapturing Constantinople from the Latins in 1261. By 1283, the Roman Sultanate as part of the civil strife and dissolved in 1308; Karamanids, another Turkish group, seized control of the Iconium sometime later.

The sultanate's collapse did not stop the conflicts between the Turks and Byzantines. The advent of a ruler, Osman (Uc Beg), led to the rise of Ottoman Beylik and the continuation of Byzantine–Ottoman clashes, which eventually resulted in the demise of the Byzantine Empire in Anatolia.

Chapter 6

The Mongol Empire

Genghis Khan (r. 1206-1227), the first Great Khan or 'universal ruler' of the Mongolians, established the Mongolian Empire (1206-1368). The Mongols were pagan. They were nomad tribes of the central Asian northern steppe who used to ride horses. At the beginning of the 13th century, they created, led and named a confederation of Turkish tribes under the leadership of Genghis Khan, which they directed toward the global expansion and spread to the East, China, in the North, Russia and Islam in the West. Through their engagement in the caravan trade, they had come to engage in everyday life just like the previous migrant groups of people like Arabs, Imazighen and Turks before them.

Genghis Khan
Mongol Emperor and Conqueror

However, they did not convert to Islam before their arrival, which was in contrast to others. In addition to that, their civilization was more sedentary, and their forces were ferocious. The culture was materialistic. They had a more complex social hierarchy and a more cohesive tribal law that have been brought with their arrival. They had a physically more devastating impact than earlier invasions and a more socially and politically creative influence in the long run.

Statue of Genghis Khan in Museum of Rockies

The beginning of Mongol incursions

A strong Mongolian commander named Temujin gathered together a majority of Mongol tribes and led them to a catastrophic sweep across China in the early years of the 13th century. He changed the name of Genghis Khan, which means "World Conqueror." In 1219, his massive army of 700,000 men was turned west, and Bukhara, Samarkand (Uzbekistan), Balkh (Afghan), Merv's capital of the ancient Seljuk Empire (today's Turkmenistan) and Neyshabur (today's Iran) quickly devastated.

In 1220, the first Mongols to foray into Islamdom was a response to a challenge from Khwārezm-Shāh ʿAlāʾ al-Dīn Muḥammad; the local governor who revolted against Seljuq's government in Khorāsān. He was the aggressive ruling monarch of a dynasty founded in the Oxus Delta. In unparalleled horror and devastation under the command of Genghis Khan, Mongolian armies demolished several Transoxania and Khorasan cities. In 1227, Genghis Khan's power extended from the Caspian Sea to the Sea of Japan by the time he died. Möngke, who succeeded the Mongolian Empire later, wanted to develop the empire in two new directions. At the same time, he sent Kublai Khan to southern China (where Islam later started growing inland) and Hülegü to Iran from the Karakorum, the Mongol capital (1256).

Khubilai Khan and his wife Chabi on a Cookout

Mongols invading Anatolia

The invasions of Anatolia by the Mongols happened between 1241 and 1255 when General Baiju from the Mongols invaded Anatolia to punish the Seljuk Sultanate of Rum for the violation of their vassal position. In 1231, the Khwarezmian Empire ended, and the Seljuk Turkish, Cilician, and Georgian empires became vassals of the Mongol empire following the killing of Khwarezmian Prince Jalal ad-Din Mingburnu. The Mongols concentrated on their conquest of Europe for ten years, but the death of Ogedei Khan weakened the empire in 1241. In 1241, Governor Baiju requested the renewal of his oath from the Seljuk sultan Kaykhusraw II. Kaykhusraw rejected and brought war by raiding another Mongol vassal, Georgia.

The Mongols pushed aside the Seljuks and marched to Erzurum, where the Seljuks insulted the emissaries of the Mongols. The Mongols, in response, retaliated and massacred the inhabitants of Erzurum, and the Mongols fled towards Georgia and Armenia to gather additional soldiers. Kaykhusraw had managed to recruit the aid of the mercenaries of Achaea, Trebizond's Empire, Ayyubids and Crusader. The Mongol army, which had 30,000 soldiers, advanced into Seljuk land in 1243 and, in June 1243, defeated the powerful force of the 60,000 Kaykhusraw's army at Kose Dag (next to Sivas), and feigned retreat before ambushing the vanguard of the Seljuk. Again, the Seljuks had to remain Mongol vassals, but the Mongols would return on a recurrent basis to exercise their control.

The Rum sultan "Ala᾽ al-Dīn Kay-Qubādh (Kaikobad) I" initiated a war against the Khwarezm dynasty of Iran in 1230, which ultimately led to the dissolution of Rum and Seljuq power. Because of the collapse of the Khorezmian buffer state, the Seljuqs could not repel the approaching Mongols when they approached Turkey's eastern borders. Seljuq autonomy was irrevocably lost in the Battle of Köse Dagh in 1243. The Seljuq sultanate remained a Mongol territory for a time, though certain Turkmen emirs established minor kingdoms of their own in remote mountainous areas. The Seljuq dynasty finally perished in the early 14th century.

Due to the collapse of the Seljuk dynasty in Rum, much of Anatolia was governed by several Anatolian beyliks by the end of the 14th century. Following fading Seljuk Sultans, the Mongols seized control of the Turkmen Beyliks. While they were subject to the Ilkhanids, the Beyliks did not issue coins in their own commanders' names. In the 1320s, the Ottoman monarch Osman I was the first Turkish leader to manufacture coins in his own name. Because issuing coins was a right granted solely to a sovereign in Islamic practice, it could be said that the Ottomans gained independence from the Mongol Khans.

Chapter 7

The Ottoman Empire

Ertugrul Bey was the son of the Suleyman Shah, chieftain of the Kayi Tribe, one of the 24 tribes of Oghuz. He was a valiant, intelligent warrior, an excellent strategist and an honest believer. The tribe of the Kayis was one of Oguz's 24 tribes, the Oghuz dynasty. He fought with his Kayi clan for several years in search of a land where his tribe could live and flourish. The Byzantine Empire had its capital in Constantinople in the 12th century. That capital is known as Istanbul today. Ertugrul Bey had been fighting with the East Roman Empire for a region where he could dwell with his people.

Ertugrul Bey

1191-1281

Mongols and the Kayi Tribe

In the meantime, the Mongolians had yet another invasion. The Mongol Empire originated in Mongolia and ultimately extended to the seas of Japan from Eastern European countries and Central Europe and was the biggest contiguous land empire in history. The Mongols rapidly reached the majority of Eastern European major cities in the late 12th century, 1237-1241. The Mongolians had invaded and burned the Ertugrul Bey's tribe. As a consequence, many individuals from Kayi Tribe had been slaughtered. Ertugrul succeeded in finding new land to live with his tribe. Despite being defeated by them, Ertugrul Bey kept giving a tough time to these Mongols. It was indeed a difficult period for the Byzantine Mongols. In the meantime, Anatolia was the last state of the Seljuk Empire which was under the rule of the most successful Sultan the Seljuk Empire had seen, Sultan Alauddin Keyoubad. He reigned the Seljuk Empire from 1222-1237.

Sultan Alauddin Keyoubad

(Last Seljuk Emperor)

Sultan Alauddin Keyoubad also had a brother named Melik Izeddin. Ertugrul Bey married Halima Sultan, the daughter of Malik Izzedin, who was one of the great rulers of the Seljuk Empire. Halima Sultan was the first and only wife of Ertugrul Bey. He is known as a Ghazi, an Islamic word for a Muslim soldier. Ertugrul Ghazi and his troop of horsemen aided the Anatolian Seljuks. His bravery and outstanding leadership laid the foundations for the Ottoman Empire.

Statue of Halima Hatun

(Wife of Ertugrul Bey)

Founder of the Ottoman Empire

Osman Bey was one of the three sons that Ertugrul had. He was the youngest among his siblings who founded the Ottoman Empire. When Osman Bey came into leadership of the Kayi tribe in Sogut, he was just 23 years old, then took over the throne after his father died. In the North West of Anatolia, Osman governed the Turkmen Principality. The name of the dynasty and the Empire he had established were taken from the Arabic name (Uthman), the spelling of his name. Osman was born quite late to his parents, Ertugrul was around 67 years old when Osman was born (1258), and Halima was older. He was regarded as a miracle of Allah (God).

Osman 1 (Osman Bey- Founder of Ottoman Empire)

1299-1323

The Ottoman Empire was one of world history's most powerful and long-lasting dynasties. For about 623 years, 1299-1923, this Islamic superpower reigned over huge regions in the Middle East, East Europe and North Africa. Bulgaria, Greece, Egypt, Jordan, Israel, Lebanon, Palestine, Macedonia, Syria, Arabia, North Africa and Romania of today were among the territories under the Ottoman Empire.

Ottomans were famous for their Art, Science and Medicine. In particular, during the reign of Sulayman the Magnificent, the tenth Sultan in the Ottoman line, Istanbul and important cities were recognized as artistic. The Muslim Empire spread and dominated the Great Wall of China and as far as Spain. The development in society and organization of this great Empire was regarded as the most advanced. Under the leadership of Osman 1, Murad 1, Orhan and Bayezid 1, the Ottoman Turks established a formal administration and extended their territory. Mehmed II, the conqueror, the 7th Ottoman sultan, led the Turks of the Ottoman Empire to take the ancient city of Constantinople in 1453. It was May 29 1453, when Constantinople fell. When the Ottomans breached the old Constantinople Wall for 57 days, the dwindling Byzantine Empire finally ended.

Sultan Mehmed II, the 7th ruler of the Ottoman Empire

Sultan Mehmed II, the 7th ruler of the Ottoman, arrived at Constantinople. He declared himself Kayser I-Rum, Rome's new Caeser, but the Ottomans will always remember him as "Faith, the Conqueror". He had persisted with his efforts for years, attempting and failing. He brought the Roman Empire to an end while he was just 21 years old.

Sultan Mehmed- 7th Sultan of Ottoman and Conqueror
1st Reign 1444-1446
2nd Reign 1451- 1481

With Constantine's fall, Constantinople had become the Ottoman Empire's capital. Mehmed II seized the city and headed to Hagia Sophia directly. It was the largest structure in all of Europe. In global history, there are only a few individuals who proclaim themselves World Conquerors. Mehmed II, the Conqueror, impacted the nature of the history of the world in numerous ways. Osman 1's ancestor was Oghuz Han/Khan, and Mehmed's ancestor was Osman I.

Istanbul, which spans Europe and Asia, is now known as Constantinople. Economic and political, the Empire which dominates it holds East and West. It was called the doorway to the world back in those days. The period of Suleiman the Magnificent is considered the Golden Period of the Ottoman Empire. Muslim and non-Muslim communities around the Mediterranean controlled much of their own affairs under the Ottomans since, in Islamic political tradition, Christians and Jews were believed to be protected. Successful governance and preservation of such a large empire required not only military power but a compromise and diplomacy as well.

Suleiman 1- The 10th Ottoman Sultan (Emperor)
Known as Suleiman. The Magnificent Sultan (Kanuni)
Reign 1520-1566

The 10th Sultan and longest-ruling of the Ottoman Empire from 1520 till his death of 1566 was Sulieman the Magnificent (known as Kanuni as he reformed the law). In times of peace, the Ottoman state governed over at least 25 million people under his leadership. Sulieman 2nd, his grandson, was one of the world's wealthiest leaders, constructing over 300 masjids (mosques) and refurbishing the Kaaba in Makkah, the walls of Jerusalem, and constructing the Suleimaniye Mosque in Istanbul. For nearly 600 years, the Ottoman Empire was the world's superpower.

Suleimaniye Masjid (Mosque)
Istanbul Masterpiece of Architect Sinan-One of the Hallmark of Istanbul

The Blue Masjid (Mosque), one of the most important works of Ottoman
History that was built by the Architect Sedefkar Mehmet Aga at the Request
of Sultan Ahmed 1, 14th Ottoman Sultan.

The fall of the Ottoman Empire

The Ottoman Empire also governed Palestine. The Ottoman Empire started collapsing after World War I, and Palestine was seized by the British in 1918. Until the civil administration was created in 1920, the British military governed Palestine. On April 25 1920, Britain received a mandate for Palestine. The State of Israel was formed on May 14 1948, an event that was of historical significance. The Middle East transformed in six days during 1967. With the capture of the Gaza and the Sinai deserts from Egypt, golden heights from Syria, the West Bank, and Jerusalem, Israel had routed the armies of Egypt, Jordan and Syria over five days.

Flag of Ottoman Empire

Hagia Sophia

Hagia Sophia has contributed to giving us many helpful insights into the time as a hub of religious, political and artistic activity in the Byzantine world. It was also a venue of Muslim worship after the conquest of Constantinople by Sultan Mehmed II in 1453. Hagia Sophia began with succeeding Byzantine architecture and, thousands of years later with the fall of Constantinople in 1453, was transformed into a Paradigmatic, Orthodox Church. The conqueror Mehmed II turned it into a mosque. In 1934, it was transformed into a museum by Mustafa Kemal Ataturk (president of Turkey). Mustafa Kemal Ataturk was a Turkish revolutionary statesman and field marshal. In 1923, he became Turkey's first president and instituted sweeping changes with the goal of establishing a new secular republic from the vestiges of its Ottoman history. After an 86-year gap, on Friday, July 24, 2020, President Tayyip Erdogan reopened Hagia Sophia as a mosque.

Hagia Sophia Museum, Istanbul

Turned in to Masjid (Mosque) 24th July 2020

List of Sultans of the Ottoman Empire

Ertugrul Bey	1. Osman 1 1299-1323	2. Orhan 1323-1362	3. Murad 1 1362-1389
7. Mehmed II The conqueror 1444-1446 1451-1481	6. Murad II 1421-1444 1446-1451	5. Mehmed 1 1413-1421	4. Byezid 1 1389-1403
8. Bayezid II 1481-1512	9. Selim 1 1512-1520	10. Sulieman the magnificent 1520-1566	11. Selim II 1566-1574
12. Murad III 1574-1595	13. Mehmed III 1595-1603	14. Ahmed 1 1603-1617	15. Mustafa 1 1617-1618 1622-1623
16. Osman II 1618-1622	17. Murad IV 1623-1640	18. Ibrahim 1640-1648	19. Mehmed IV 1648-1687
23. Ahmed III 1703-1730	22. Mustafa II 1695-1703	21. Ahmed II 1691-1695	20. Suleiman II 1687-1691
24. Mahmud 1 1730-1754	25. Osman III 1754-1754	26. Mustafa III 1757- 1774	27. Abdul Hamid 1774-1789
31. Abdul Mejid 1839-1861	30. Mahmud II 1808-1839	29. Mustafa IV 1807-1808	28. Selim III 1789-1807

32. Abdul Aziz 1861-1876	33. Abdul Hamid 2 1876-1909	34. Mehmed V 1909-1918	35. Mehmed VI 1918-1922
36. Abdul Mejid 2 1922-1924			

Glossary

Aga	Military Commander/Leader
Alp	A masculine hero of strength and courage
Agha	Chief Military Officer
Bey/Beg/Baig/Begh	Commander/General (Bey is originally a Turkish name. It is spelt differently in different countries)
Beylik	Owner of Estate
Beylerbey	A provincial governor
Begum	Female variant of Bey
Baba	Father also known as Holy man
Caliphate/Khilafah	Chief Muslim ruler
Constantinople	Now Istanbul
Daulah	Arabic Dynasty of state
Emir/Amir	Commander or Prince
Gazi	Warrior of the faith
Han/Khan	Turkish Khan meaning ruler or chief
Islam	Submission to the will of Allah (God)
Madrasa	Islamic college usually attached to a Mosque or Masjid
Mahdi	The rightly guided one, to rule before the end of the world
Malik	Arabic King
Mufti	Islamic Juror
Mullah	Islamic dignity scholar
Mirza	Persian origin rank of Royal Prince, High Nobleman, Distinguished Military Commander or Scholar
Muslim	People who follow Islam
Nawab	Deputy Ruler

Pasha	High civic or military officer
Pashalik	Territory under a provincial pasha rule
Rum	The area ruled by Byzantine Empire/Roman East Empire
Sultan	Ruler/King
Sunnah	Social and legal practice of the Prophet Muhammad (S.A.W)
Shah	Persian King
Timar	Military stipend
Timariot	Horseman holding a Timar
Turk	Son of Japheth
Vizier	Royal Minister
Ummah	Muslim community

The Prophet Muhammad's (PBUH) Last Sermon

This sermon was delivered on the Ninth day of Dhul-Hijjah 10 A.H, in the Uranah valley of Mount Arafat.

After praising and thanking Allah, he said:

"O, People! Lend me an attentive ear, for I know not whether after this year I shall ever be amongst you again. Therefore, listen carefully to what I am saying and take these words to those who could not be present here today."

"O People! Just as you regard this month, this day, this city as Sacred, so regard the life and property of every Muslim a sacred trust. Return the goods entrusted to you to their rightful owners. Hurt no one so that no one may hurt you. Remember that you will indeed meet your Lord and that he will indeed reckon your deeds."

"Allah has forbidden you to take usury; therefore, all interest obligation shall henceforth be waived. Your capital is yours to keep. You will neither inflict nor suffer any inequality.

"Allah has judged that there shall be no interest and that all interest due to Abbas Ibn' Aal-Muttalib be waived."

"Every right arising out of homicide in pre-Islamic days is henceforth waived, and the first such right that I waive is that arising from the murder of Rabiah ibn al-Harithiah."

"O men! The unbelievers indulge in tampering with the calendar in order to make permissible that which Allah forbade and to prohibit what Allah has made permissible. With Allah, the months are twelve in number. Four of them are holy, there are successive, and one occurs singly between the months of Jumada and Shaban."

"Beware of Satan, for the safety of your religion. He has lost all hope that he will be able to lead you astray in big things, so beware of following him in small things."

"O People, it is true that you have certain rights with regard to your women, but they also have rights over you. Remember that you have taken them as your wives only under Allah's trust and with His permission. If they abide by your right, then to them belongs the right to be fed and clothed in kindness. Do treat your women well and be kind to them, for they are your partners and committed helpers. And it is your right that they do not make friends with anyone of whom you do not approve, as well never to be unchaste."

"O People! Listen to me in earnest, worship Allah, say your five daily prayers, fast during the month of Ramadan, and give your wealth in Zakat. Perform Hajj if you can afford it."

"All mankind is from Adam and Eve, an Arab has no superiority over a non-Arab nor a non-Arab has any superiority over an Arab; also a White has no superiority over a Black nor does a Black have any superiority over a White except by piety and good action. Learn that every Muslim is a brother to every Muslim and that the Muslims constitute one brotherhood. Nothing shall be legitimate to a Muslim which belongs to a fellow Muslim unless it was given freely and willingly."

"Do not, therefore, do injustice to yourselves. Remember, one day, you will meet Allah and answer your deeds. So beware, do not stray from the path of righteousness after I am gone."

"O, People! No Prophet or apostle will come after me, and no new faith will be born. Reason well, therefore, O People! And understand words that I convey to you. I leave behind me two things, the Quran and the Sunnah, and if you follow these, you will never go astray."

"All those who listen to me shall pass on my words to others and those to others again, and may the last ones understand my words better than those who listen to me directly."

"O Allah, be my witness that I have conveyed your message to your people."

Question:

You were named Bey, Beg or Baig. How do you know if your forefather is Oghuz?

Answered by Mohim Baig:

My research and study have found that people who strongly believe in faith and their clan are hurt or attacked; they can instantly feel it. The Oghuz have been attacked, too. Whether they lived in a different country or lived nearby, they are reunited quickly and help each other physically and politically. They always stand against cruelty, injustice and are always ready to fight and regroup with their clan. Justice has to be done by any means, and when you serve humanity for that justice, you know that your forefather is Oghuz.

TO LAWRANCE

Thank You

Assalamu Alaikum Wa - Rahmatullahi
May the peace Mercy of Allaah be **with you**

Sign by Author
Mohim Baig

Mohim Baig

17 - 08 - 2022

Printed in Great Britain
by Amazon